W0259628

'In this thrilling collection of sonnets, Leo Boix maps a personal geography out of dynamic encounters between the Old World and the New, between sweeping landscapes and miniature, as he brilliantly captures the fluctuations of history, the natural world and the inner self. A splendid testament to Alexander von Humboldt's own scientific vision and boundless curiosity, and his theory that everything is interconnected, everything interacts, every existence is part of a joyous and fragile totality' – Chloe Aridjis

'As Terrance Hayes recast the American sonnet for the twenty-first century, Leo Boix captures the spirit of Argentina in this vibrant, formally adroit and compelling sequence. *Southernmost* is a vivid, transhemispheric memoir of queer love, loss and migration that casts its dazzling, occasionally Gothic spell on wherever it alights, from the shores of the South Atlantic to the English Channel. Generous, vulnerable and vivifying' – Karen McCarthy Woolf

'Leo Boix's cartographic sonnets give queer form to interlocking personal and social histories, making music of loss and displacement. Their diasporic intellect summons "Latin America's heart" with equal parts rigour and play in a poetics as sinuous and expansive as the ocean between us'

– Urayoán Noel

SOUTHERNMOST: SONNETS

Leo Boix

Chatto & Windus
LONDON

1 3 5 7 9 10 8 6 4 2

Chatto & Windus, an imprint of Vintage, is part of the Penguin Random House group of companies

Vintage, Penguin Random House UK, One Embassy Gardens, 8 Viaduct Gardens, London SW11 7BW

penguin.co.uk/vintage
global.penguinrandomhouse.com

First published by Chatto & Windus in 2025

Typeset in 11/14pt Minion Pro by Jouve (UK), Milton Keynes
Printed and bound in Great Britain by Clays Ltd, Elcograf S.p.A.

The authorised representative in the EEA is Penguin Random House Ireland, Morrison Chambers, 32 Nassau Street, Dublin D02 YH68

A CIP catalogue record for this book is available from the British Library

ISBN 9781784745851

Penguin Random House is committed to a sustainable future for our business, our readers and our planet. This book is made from Forest Stewardship Council® certified paper.

Contents

It was at the far edge of the far edge
about to exist and about not to exist like faith.

– Cristina Rivera Garza

As a boy in Argentina, I used to collect all sorts of things –
dried and pinned local insects, Latin American stamps,
ferns in clay pots, shells from our seaside house, strings
of various colours, stones, hand-coloured atlases and maps.
My aunt Susi, Mother's only sister, would introduce me
to many varieties, from the bright-orange Monarch butterfly
and the larvae of astylus beetles to the Andes' rarest bees.
My bedroom would turn laboratory, and I'd start to classify.
So when you brought me Gerard's *Herball* for my birthday
and told me it was the most famous of all English botanicals,
I thought of him leaning down to look at a rare plant display,
like I did, collecting items so that one day I'd be immortal.
Borges wrote about it in 'Tlön, Uqbar, Orbis Tertius' – a world
conjured out of an encyclopedia, a rose that starts to unfurl.

I

I cross transparencies as though I were blind,
a reflection erases me, I'm born in another,
oh forest of pillars that are enchanted

– Octavio Paz

1

In the yellowed picture of early 1976, she spoon-feeds me,
first tasting herself before it's my turn. She holds on
to a white dish of hot, mushy stuff. She wears a carmine
summer dress, her black hair tied back in a small chignon.
She sits in a picnic chair by a low folding table with a flask,
a maté mug, and yerba in a plastic tub. I'm bathed in sunshine,
half her body is under the shade of an ombú. Her face is the mask
of a southern Aphrodite looking straight at me, her bloodline.
This is one of the few snapshots of her I brought from Argentina –
a relic of us, captured in that instant of me being nourished,
a hand about to feed the infant; a photo coated with a patina
of gold, framed over my writing table, she, the adored
empress. A rare survival here in diaspora, a *memento vivere*
where everything began for me – a life's premiere.

2

Pink iguanas on the volcano's slopes felt the tremor –
everything shook, the red crabs hid under the rocks
while the Galapagos penguins dived in together.
The exodus began, and it persisted like aftershocks.
The tallest mountain had erupted, spewing lava down
its flank. Huge clouds of ash spread over the Pacific,
miles away from everywhere, rising like a crown
of dust over the islands and beyond, surging, prolific.
I saw tortoises roaming free in the calderas of Alcedo,
after travelling to Cerro Azul, Darwin and Sierra Negra –
too slow to catch up with anything, somehow delayed
by time, space, evolution and also by the idyllic Sierra.
My eyes fixed on the glowing lava piercing through
the pre-dawn darkness, pumice in the deepest blue.

3

I see her seated in her favourite garden chair, bathed
by a sub-tropical sun. She's surrounded by big succulents
growing in clay pots. She looks absent or perhaps dazed
by the Spring heat, the jazmín del país scent, its opulence.
She touches her growing belly. Soon, a baby boy will come.
I see her talking to him through that invisible veil, a membrane
that moves as she whispers. She tells him secrets. Her thumb
caresses the stretching skin, its arc, before dozing off again.
I tiptoe to her, try not to wake her up. She's dreaming
about the October baby. A white strand overlays her black hair.
I want to tell her not to worry, that although long after the birthing,
her blood will turn poisoned, he'll sing to her from another chair
in a hospital south of Buenos Aires, songs to alleviate her pain,
songs she sang to him as a little boy, of maidens, frogs and rain.

4

I'm trying to explain myself again, but to no avail.
We're having family dinner at home. Mother
sits next to me. Father stares opposite. A red snail
comes out of my mouth. And there's much laughter.
Both sisters look at me in disbelief. *What is he saying?*
After the snail, a spotted harlequin frog blurts out
as I speak, and then a bird of paradise, now jumping
over the table. Father is getting impatient. He shouts.
Then, Mother begins to translate. She tells the family
what I am trying to say as I look at her, at my animals
making havoc between meat plates and a bowl of celery.
She recounts my story. And they become tameable.
Years later, in another country, I'll be an interpreter
who tries to render things from one world to another.

5

At the back of the winding house where grandmother was born,
grandfather kept all sorts of rabbits inside a home-made cage –
there were American rabbits with pink eyes and ears like horns,
and also the light brown and highly nervous Belgian Hares.
There were the Dutch rabbits too, but they became depressed
after spending too much time inside their crate. Grandfather
hand-fed them every day and counted them. Yet, some escaped
through holes they dug after it rained, which made him despair.
One night he said he'd had enough of all the dammed rabbits
and sold them to a local butcher, who in turn came one day
and wrapped them in burlap bags. The neighbours were upset
at the parting of the sinless bunnies, all ready to be slain.
With all that money grandfather bought some fancy chickens,
which he killed on Saturdays by swiftly twisting their lovely necks.

6

A golden forest floats away from the low islands –
a rare patchwork quilt buoyed by copious air sacks –
and as the sun shines on its bladders, diamonds
like white gooseberries gleam. Crabs ride on its back.
An ocean without a coastline sailing between seas,
the rootless sargassum drifts aimlessly, guarding
the seawater's bosom against the invading thieves
as it moves along with warm currents, ever-shifting.
Christopher Columbus once got caught in its tongs
on his way to the 'baja mar', *Bahamas*, his feeble ships
embraced by the clutching seaweed, like sirens' songs
seeking to divert them from their dark, conquering trip.
He feared they would face the same fate as past sailors,
trapped in a solid sea that held ships like sea monsters.

7

My step-grandmother, a provincial blue-blooded woman,
told me that long ago, as a rural teacher, she met Evita
at her palace in Avenida 9 de Julio. There was friction
on that first encounter. And on her desk: Aqua vitae.
She said Perón's wife was already dying, her pale face
glowing, her lips tight as her bleached chignon.
She said Evita told her she despised the upper classes,
the rich old families of Buenos Aires, all their minions.
Then, the First Lady of Argentina asked my step-granny
what she needed. *Things for my school, clothes, books,*
any equipment, whatever you could give us. She agreed
with a sneer and took out her leather-bound chequebook.
Step-grandmother always remembered that tense conclave
and often said Eva Perón was as generous as class vindictive.

8

(Francisco de Goya, *The Sleep of Reason Produces Monsters*, 1797–99)

All Latin American demons came at night; first, El Cuco,
to remind me I was still a misbehaving child, to kidnap me
in his bag. Then it was El Sombrerón from Pernambuco,
braiding the tail of a black horse, warning me not to flee.
After him, Acalica from a cave in Bolivia, a weather-fairy
who came to whisper about mother's untimely illness.
La Llorona was next, yelling for her drowned kids, wary
of my snoring, my nakedness. She was the crying witness.
All of them in a procession, to keep my insomnia going,
aware that after midnight my fears would be insignificant,
that in my dreams all monsters merged together, glowing
over my small bed where I tried to sleep in spite of visitants.
I often saw those monsters hovering above my head, omens
of a life that would come, of tragedies, journeys, and oceans.

9

The world's smallest armadillo, the so-called pichiciego,
lives, like the great Incubus, hidden in the underworld.
Armed in a majestic cloak from the head down, he burrows
deep in the arid soil, where he holes up for hours in a curl.
He didn't fight a futile war in the freezing South Atlantic,
nor die buried, scared and alone, on a far-off foreign island.
Hairless, voluptuous, with a bony carapace, he has satanic
little eyes that glow brightly at night. On the Pampas land,
he smells danger – armed hunters, foxes, the wildest boars –
before tunnelling through the ground as fast as a small fish
into the murky sea floor. For him, there are no closed doors.
He remains unflappable, crossing the dusty tracks. I wish
he'd camouflage better, take advantage of his Lilliputian size,
to remain king of the endless Patagonia, always in disguise.

10

After mother urged my father to do more male bonding
with his only son, he finally took me to a football match.
And off we went. We travelled to Nuñez on a bus carrying
a big River Plate flag. I was wearing the club's T-shirt, hat.
It was my first time in a big stadium and I didn't fit in.
The queues, the endless chanting, the dirty chorizo vans
outside. Everyone in macho mood, virile, and I wasn't even
nine. I didn't know the game's rules, yet was dressed as a fan.
Then the match kicked off. A massive roar. What was that?
Already a goal? Or was it an off-side? Father looked at me,
sort of half-smiled. He already knew, or perhaps thought
that I was too sensitive, too close to my sisters' dollies.
We didn't talk on the way home. The match was lost.
Father promised to take me back again, but he did not.

11

In our small courtyard in Buenos Aires, a falso cafeto grew
out of nothing. It appeared on a tiny patch of soil and grass
where mother used to hang all our wet clothes and shoes
to dry, a forgotten place in the far reaches of our house.
The tree of greyish bark shot up fast, its long palmate
leaves gave us kids shade. We even hung a seesaw from it
that father built with ropes and wood from an old pallet.
Yet on its first summer its green seedpods swelled, split,
and scattered over the flagstones; the place was a minefield
of spikes that dried under the sun. The false coffee tree
didn't live long. Father had had enough of it and sealed
its fate one day of intense heat after he cut his big bare feet.
Later, I learned the falso cafeto was sacred to the Guaraní,
that they danced barefoot under it, entranced and holy.

12

Mother sits by the cooking burner, ready to be transported far.
She chops sweet onions for the weekly pot. The radio haunts
the smokey place. It plays a bolero by Gatica: 'Somos'. We are.
She sings quietly along to her favourite tune. He wants
to talk. The dog sleeps under the kitchen table. He's wary
and doesn't know where to start. He met a boy. They kissed
behind grandfather's closet. In an instant. His old dirty
shoes by the dog, her stained apron over her thin wrist.
The small yellow kitchen's bright lamp undoes him. Right
away, Mother senses his stare. Dinner isn't ready yet.
He wants to say things, but he can't. A big storm lights
up the night, water overflows the lead gutters. A threat
takes everything away – subtropical leaves, twigs, slime,
a smooth, pale blue strand. We don't have much time.

13

Outside a small hovel shared by many families,
a pregnant woman gathers guava leaves, a potage
for her two-year-old son. She foresees calamities
looming wider over her run-down Quibo village.
On the Beni River, people are losing their memory.
They feel eels are eating their insides, unchained,
their tongues have turned black. There's no remedy
for the wild malady that plagues them, young or aged.
Gold mines have bloomed from the lethal waterways.
Fish feed on mercury. Their eyes shine red and sinister.
They swim upstream in a frenzy, then copulate in bays
of wickedness, ending up as supper for the villagers.
One day the whole town gathers to see the miracle –
a three-headed calf born at night, their ghastly oracle.

14

(Leonor Fini, *Autoportrait au Scorpion*, 1938)

She looks straight at us with that defiant gaze of hers.
Her hair is up with big hazel curls, her sculpted curls.
She's had her hair done and told an elderly coiffeur
about a recurrent dream of a dying Argentinean girl.
As she's about to leave, she puts her little grey gloves on,
gloves of soft suede that suddenly catch the last light;
the same pearly gloves hide her secret, the scorpion
filled with venom to defend herself. She's ready to bite.
Unlike Mother, whose biting pincers were taken away
for her own good, the day Father and Doctor decided
not to tell her about her deadly illness and then prayed
for her health to improve. That's exactly what they did.
Like Leonor Fini in her self-portrait, was she also defiant
as she faced her final hour, or was she willing, compliant?

The Crown of the Virgin

Mother prays to Nuestra Señora del Sagrado Corazón.
She kneels down, her long hands touch her sore lips.
She's saying something to herself, and whispers alone
before the crowned virgin, a holy belt above her hips.
I am next to her, looking at her stark profile, her rosary,
the way she rubs each rose-scented bead, how she kisses
the metal cross. A choir begins to sing. Above the sacristy
a neon sign flickers: *Blessed Is The Fruit of Thy Womb: Jesus.*
Then someone plays a guitar, the congregation joins in,
mother stands up, holds my hand, half-smiles at me as if
to say we're nearly there, *You've done quite well,* within
the church Sunday mass is wrapping up, what a relief.
And when we leave the priest concludes: God be with you –
Vayan con Dios. Outside a legless man begs along the queue.

Vayan con Dios. Outside a legless man begs along the queue.
He gets a coin or two, a piece of bread, a 5 pesos bill note.
Mother drives her Citroen thinking of our Sunday barbecue:
we kids play cards in the back, sing Church songs, and joke
about the old man who slept through the entire service
snoring like a bear, and the choir boy called Juan, who sang
as if he was about to die. Later at our house, father serves us
asado he cooked while we prayed, tender meat that shrank
from thick bones. Before we eat, a blessing to the virgin
and her crowned son. Mother looks at her sweaty husband,
thanks him for the food we're about to eat, curses the sins
of this world. We cross ourselves hastily and I'm damned.
As a centrepiece, a large Capodimonte vase of roses adorns
the family table. On the wall, Jesus & his crown of thorns.

The family table. On the wall, Jesus & his crown of thorns.
My unloved catechesis books. Thoughts after confessing.
The priest hugs me alone in a small chapel. He performs
the godly rites, asks if I've sinned. It's all about suppressing
bad thoughts: *tell him, tell him.* The virgin watches, thinks
perhaps I'm lying, that the priest is rubbing his toned leg
against mine. He wants to know it all, his babyish cheeks
smell of brine, *tell him tell him.* His small eyes, two blue eggs.
Then he makes me pray. *You'll be a good boy.* Un buen chico.
Too many flowers have decomposed. Sun is out. I'm not
praying as I should have. All I can think of is naked Nico
behind the classroom curtains, dancing like an astronaut.
That night Jesus arrives in my dream and softly hugs me,
his big heart bleeds red wax & I drink from the almighty.

His big heart bleeds red wax & I drink from the almighty.
Figuratively, that is. All day at school we start to learn
about the life of the Virgin, what to pray on Good Fridays,
about the Old & New Testament, when Christ returned
from the afterlife bearing bleeding holes on each hand.
In our classroom in a big, framed photo, John Paul II,
making the sign of the cross, half-smiles, is content
in spite of his mitre, his crosses, his yellow cretonnes.
Soon, my First Holy Communion. I duly prepare
by going to the local cathedral, rehearsing in line
how to receive the sacramental bread, Christ's affair,
his body in our bodies. I'm the purest boy by nine.
After the service they take a picture of me praying:
I'm looking up to Him; me, the angelic boy, betraying.

I'm looking up to Him; me, the angelic boy, betraying
the Holy Scriptures, with the face of some Devil,
praying at Christmas mass, at Easter's, promising
never to come back to Church again, to settle
for a Godless life. The little angelito is now standing
in front of the crowned virgin of the sacred heart,
looking at men kneeling in their tight jeans, bending
to take the holy eucharist, to receive Him like a dart,
And lead us not into temptation, but deliver us from evil,
the priest with his arms stretched out, a thick beard,
his golden robes, a bright green maniple with tassels,
how he kisses the altar boys like two sweet birds.
The Son of God made answer as only humans can.
With arms outstretched he bid me 'Come first to me as man'.

With arms outstretched, he bids me *Come first to me as man*,
and I do come to him and he asks me what is wrong
with me, and I can't say. All I want to do is run
away from him. He says the Lord will make me strong.
And I pray to the crowned virgin and her little son,
to the bleeding heart and the saintly nun, turn this boy
into a man, wash my sins, forgive me for what I've done.
Then the bearded man kisses my lips & I am full of joy.
That day my friend Ivan comes to our house to play,
we get naked in my tiny bedroom and it is electric,
and he says don't tell anyone, it'll be our secret. Away
he goes and a big storm appears. It feels magnetic.
My spirit's search for union / And my body's strong desire /
Unite in this sweet moment, / To light the sacred fire.

Unite in this sweet moment, to light the sacred fire,
the priest recites from the pulpit. Mother watches me
looking at the blond lad, a never-ending prayer.
Two elderly women cry near the altar's canopy.
We pretend nothing happens. His face is bleeding
from his crown of thorns. The priest lifts his hand,
crosses himself and we cross ourselves after him.
Mass is over but we remain. Inside, the choir chants
as I look at Mother next to me, her ailing body,
how she prays to stay with us, begs from all the saints
she knows. She prays for me, for us, while a Pavarotti-
looking man sings a holy psalm about human fate.
She kisses her rosary, wishes for me not to be alone.
Mother prays to Nuestra Señora del Sagrado Corazón.

16

Don Juan Díaz de Solís, looking for a new passage
to the Far East, entered the Río de la Plata basin.
He named it Mar Dulce, *Sweet Sea*, but the savages
got his sailors first, then him, and all were eaten.
It all occurred in the first month of February, 1516.
A town called Santa María de los Buenos Ayres
was founded a few years later, a low site of mean
aspect, decrepit, muddy, full of spirits, bad fairies.
Then three years later, the Spaniards fell again.
Not much to be done. The place lay abandoned
as native Charrúas closed in and burnt it all down,
those little flimsy houses. All the locals murdered.
A place forever cursed, they must have thought,
as they left behind the tenuous city, a flaming spot.

17

Father drives his yellow car to the Mercado Central
at the end of the 25 de Mayo motorway. He tells us
the names of all the city neighbourhoods: San Cristóbal,
Constitución, Almagro, Boedo, Liniers, Floresta, Flores,
while mother sings boleros we know from the radio,
us children in the back seat looking at the windowsills
from above, the cramped balconies, the large stadium,
the rickety trucks and old colectivos left behind. The thrill
of arriving at the city's largest market with our empty bags,
of buying as many vegetables, as much meat as we could
fit in the car. We queue for hours and look at price tags,
try to fill our car's boot with the knockdown goods.
Back home, we switch on the old TV and watch Road Runner
about to be eaten by a famished coyote. It always backfires.

18

My headteacher mother loved her telenovelas at teatime.
She watched curled up, the famous one about a poor orphan
who ended up marrying the rich heartthrob, even despite
knowing he was her blood brother, and she his fortune.
I'd watch mother sit bewitched, facing the television set.
Often by her side, a big pot full of green beans to be peeled,
her school papers, a lighter, a pack of her long slim cigarettes.
An afternoon immersed in other people's miseries and duels.
Sometimes she'd lament and talk about that wronged girl,
always unlucky in love, tricked, desperate for a final change;
how she'd escape to a large tropical house, a far-away world
where fate could shift so suddenly, and a new life arranged.
She got used to the ridiculous plots, the twists and turns,
and after watching for an hour, she'd plan the school terms.

19

When godmother lost her newborn baby, nobody cried
or perhaps they did. The house turned gelid. No one spoke
of the evil spell. A witch doctor came to us and warned
against letting sunlight in. Godmother wore a black cloak,
forgot to pray, lit candles to all her saints, sang odd lullabies
where wolves appeared behind tall trees and ate boys' flesh
like in a kingly feast. The Gargantuan kitchen was full of flies.
The crib was taken to the basement, along with the lace dress.
Nobody spoke about it, or maybe they did. A ghost remained
behind great-grandfather's cupboard, his tiny fingers happily
tapping as they wound back the clocks. The unexplained
events mounted in that house once built by an immigrant family.
They say she was always unlucky, that she attracted bad luck,
that instead of smiling as a child she'd always frown and sulk.

20

Aleixo García reached the land between Tomina and Mizque,
in what is today Bolivia. There, he loaded up his treasure:
fine cloths, jewellery, and many artefacts of gold, silver, zinc.
The first European to find the riches of the Inca empire,
he went back to tell the world of his trove. Though he arrived
safely on the Paraguay River's shores, he would get no further.
'He was murdered by the barbarians', a Jesuit described,
'who took his Inca hoard. They were all Guaraní warriors'.
It reminds me of that time grandmother told us children
a story about a local robber who one day raided grandfather's
shop and was, in turn, robbed by his vengeful wife, a Brazilian.
She said it was all God's making to punish the first burglar.
Quien roba a un ladrón, tiene cien años de perdón, she warned us –
Whoever steals from a thief has a hundred years of forgiveness.

21

My aunt fears all subtropical winters, sharpened shears,
big stray dogs when they bark, the unbearable violence
of police sirens as they howl and howl. She always fears
her snoopy neighbours, rickety buses, electric fences.
My aunt fears financial decrees, military tombstones,
the vivid memory of herself as a young student burying
books by Che Guevara, Marx, Trotsky, Lenin, Eva Perón,
deep in her parents' courtyard garden, secretly kneeling
like a blindfolded hostage to be shot. She recalls it all
as if it had happened to someone else, a doppelgänger,
herself, a two-faced impostor. She fears unexpected calls,
big moustaches, dictators in leather boots, big daggers.
She fears being sunk by her fears like a young soft body
still alive and breathing, but drugged, thrown into the sea.

22

Father parks his yellow Peugeot outside the hospital,
turns off the radio, and looks at Mother. Estás lista?
Are you ready? She nods, touches her hair just a little,
and presses her handbag with a letter from the specialist.
They sit silently in the waiting room, hold hands
until they're called in. The doctor looks at the spots
on the X-ray and asks my mother to please stand
outside while both men decide to tell her or not
about her blood condition, that she might have a year
or two left with luck. Father tells the doctor she has three
young children and is a headteacher. She doesn't hear
as both men decide not to tell her after all. They're free
to go. *It's nothing serious*, he says to her at the doorway.
She smiles her quiet smile, and then he speeds away.

23

In a dense forest of the Gran Chaco, *the hunting land*,
Argentina's largest jaguar – the Qaramtá – is on high patrol
and goes for giant anteaters, tapirs, capybaras and lambs.
He's crouched down by the riverbed, alert, in full control.
Close by, a guide on horseback pulls a boat with tourists.
He splashes and swims in the stinking brown lagoons
until we're all in a raised settlement surrounded by a forest.
The whole place is an oven, it's already late in the afternoon.
I could be Qaramtá, staring at them from a hiding place, blurred
by the dense hot thicket. The place is named El Impenetrable,
almost impossible to enter. But we're all here for the jaguar,
its coat of amber fur, its black rosette-shaped spots, the muscled
god of South America. Then we see him, his feline physique,
eyes staring at us as in flames, *he who kills with one leap.*

24

The very first Englishman to explore all the Americas
discovered that Tierra del Fuego, the mythical land south
of the Magellan Strait, wasn't a continent, as Europeans
thought, but a group of islands in the shape of a mouth.
'We, with Divine assistance, were hungrie to saile thither to the Pacifik,
to make a perfect discovery of the same'. Two years on, they'd 'gotten
a pretty store of money'. The English pirate was prolific:
you can read of Drake's adventures in many Elizabethan sonnets.
He sailed on the *Pelican*, which he renamed at one of his meals
the *Golden Hind,* and after conquering the monstrous waves
for many years, he returned to London with all his spoils
and dined with Elizabeth on board his ship by the Thames.
Drake danced with the Queen to the tune of fourteen lutes.
She later knighted him for his plunder, his courage, his looks.

25

Father took us that summer to Rio de Janeiro,
the whole family stayed at one of the best hotels.
We ate gargantuan breakfasts, wore sombreros,
climbed the mighty Corcovado, gathered shells
at the Copacabana beach. We were in paradise.
He was desperate for us to have the greatest time,
spent all the money he had, took us to high-priced
restaurants, shops, bought mother the most sublime
cocktail dress, onyx earrings and toys for us. Later,
I learnt that before the summer started, he was told
mother had months to live. A trip to enrapture her,
discovering a Brazilian heaven of sand and gold.
It all felt to us so light, hot and sensuous, the levity
of not knowing, or somehow sensing life's brevity.

26

There was a pine at the end of our street, a huge monster
called Mañío macho. Police cars went round in circles, sharks
of dark blue light, always on patrol. Every morning, a beggar
or two, singing cumbias. My sister with a wrong birthmark.
The moon used to grow gigantic, and it reddened. It appeared
above the murky River Plate. We often called it *la luna macabra.*
The buildings in town had mouths and ears. We whispered
to them all magic words, but no answers. Was it *abracadabra*?
Once, a witch woman (la curandera) touched a child's back
with a measuring tape, counted the days left of a hidden serpent.
There were flowers the size of giant hands, and spiders. At dusk,
some locals painted their faces with white chalk, like insurgents.
I remember pyres made of old tyres, furious flames whirled.
The fire tall enough to be seen from the other side of the world.

27

When mother fell ill we went on a pilgrimage
to see Our Lady of the Rosary of San Nicolás.
We took her to see the chapel, the vicarage,
and she wanted to pray, kneeling during mass.
She bought a holy card of the sacred virgin
with the message: 'May your presence ease
my being burdened by sickness and suffering.'
She placed a candle by the virgin's altarpiece.
She later worsened and couldn't walk anymore.
I sang her favourite songs for the pain to go away
but the pain never went, it grew as never before.
The praying intensified, more pills on her tray.
Was she thinking of the virgin as she passed?
What did she see as she died?

28

Nocturnal bird of the Atacama desert, you shine bright
on the crispiest of nights as you take flight from the dunes.
Your wings glow a metallic hue; your eyes radiate a rare light
of gold and silver from nearby mines. They say you're a moon
surging from the Southern Hemisphere, a shooting star, a flash,
the sole guide of farmer Juan Godoy to the rich silver outcrops
of Chañarcillo, an event that sparked the Chilean silver rush.
Some say you are made of green copper, of entire sundrops.
I saw you once as a boy in the golden sierras outside Merlo,
near where El Algarrobo Abuelo, the ancient carob tree was,
you were taking flight as the night was falling, hovering low
by the tree, glowing like a hanging lantern in a land of gods.
There you turned to me and shone, oh mythical Alicanto,
and I suddenly saw below mountaintops, myself *muy alto* . . .

29

In his *First Voyage around the Globe* of 1524,
the bold Italian nobleman Antonio Pigafetta
writes about how Magellan, the avid explorer,
landed one rough winter in Southern Patagonia,
how he tricked two Tehuelches, shackled them
for a 'collection of unusual specimens' given
to the teenage Spanish Emperor. He named them
Patagonians, after a known character, a medieval
giant with big feet and a monstrous appearance.
'Their faces were large and painted cardinal . . .
and they had two hearts painted on their ears.'
Many believe that Shakespeare's famous Caliban,
the son of Sycorax, was born out of the Italian's
stark portrait of those two unfortunate native men.

30

(The Unholy Family)

At least as unholy as my mother, she brought me home
wrapped in newspaper sheets. Bad news this time. Born
before disaster struck. Father killed impure pups, foam
spilled from buckets of black water. Young sister burned
dolls, old sister run away on a truck. Our manger collapsed
under a star taking us nowhere. Family fled to a desert
mounted on a giant rat covered in velvet. Time elapsed,
we travelled awhile, mother left us. Our legs on high alert.
Then real exodus began: I learnt to be a cursed witch
on a stick, took a few song birds, untranslatable books,
wrote back endless letters as my mouth got more stitches.
They called me once, twice. Stopped. I died near a brook.
It all happened a long time ago, no one now remembers this story:
let me tell you how it all happened, how we turned unholy.

31

For my 18th, wicked stepmother took me to the Ballet.
Sleeping Beauty at Teatro Colón, the gilded opera house
in Buenos Aires. We had dinner at Edelweiss with Strauss
playing emphatically in the background. All the gay
balletomanes were there, and a group of American tourists.
The acoustics in the theatre astonished, as boys sighed
with emotion. Large women stared through binoculars, dyed
chignons adorned with neon flowers from an enchanted forest.
It was summer, and the strapping male dancers in tights
were sweating like South American pigs. Their genitals
enlarged in those padded belts. Their legs flaying like tentacles
over stepmother, as she bravoed through their tropical flight.
She drove me back to our house in the northern suburbs,
and later in bed, I dreamt of men in leotards, dancing bluebirds.

32

At Ave Porco in Calle Corrientes in Buenos Aires,
fat pinkish pigs hung above the dance floor
with wings and painted faces like Zsa Zsa Gabor.
On all the adjoining walls, the most jarring series
of murals with more flying pigs, frills and glitter
and in the middle of it all, the largest mirror-ball
under which drag queens, dressed as Barbie dolls,
danced the drugs away in ecstasy with their dealers.
I was there in 1993, where I met my first boyfriends,
until one night, the iconic place announced its end,
and all the revellers were invited to nicely pull down
the whole bar and take home the place's contents.
It was like the Berlin Wall had fallen, as all the kids
went souvenir mad, fighting over the fat hanging pigs.

33

When the Ballets Russes embarked on a South American tour in August 1913, there was trouble on the horizon. Diaghilev was unhappy. In the party, there was Mrs Pulszky, a self-assured Catholic aristocrat from Hungary who fell in love with Vaslav Nijinsky, even though he was apparently a rabid homosexual. She duly prayed for his conversion, referred to him as *Le Petit*, all she wanted was his baby. She chased him like an irrational man-eater, booked herself into an adjoining cabin and got ready to bump into him in the corridors, on deck and at mealtimes. She even befriended his hot masseur for inside information. Though she was told of his affair with Diaghilev, his sex crimes, she succeeded in getting a proposal after much persuasion. When the couple arrived in Argentina, they went straight away to get married. After the union, a friend wrote: *It was all so gay!*

34

'There, we built a new town and called it Bonas Aeieres
that is, in our German, *Guter Wind,* though the air was vile.
From Hispania, we brought livestock: 72 horses and mares.
Here, also, we found a place inhabited by an Indian tribe.
They brought us fish and meat to eat. These Querandíes
have no houses, but wander about, as do the Gipsies
with us at home . . . and when they meet with wild deer
and other beasts, they drink their blood, and get tipsy.
And when they first came to our town, Bonas Aeieres,
and attacked us, some of them tried to storm the town,
others shot fiery arrows at our straw-covered houses,
which were set on fire, and the whole place burnt down.'
As written by Ulderico Schmidt, the German adventurer,
who joined Pedro de Mendoza's expedition to get richer.

35

After finishing high school, I decided to travel solo
through South America. I first flew to the Altiplano,
crisscrossed Bolivia on rickety buses, and although
I had no schedule, I knew I wanted to see the volcanoes
of the Galapagos. I crossed to Peru, to the town of Puno,
where I met two Chileans who, like me, were journeying
through our vast continent, trying to find who knows
what: the perfect ruin, the mightiest forest, a rare bird, taking
our time to move from place to place. Until I reached Ecuador
and spent a night alone in a tiny hut by the Pacific, and all
I could see were stars through holes in the roof – Ursa Major,
the Big Dipper, the Southern Cross. The sky, a spluttered shawl.
And I realised I couldn't go on travelling; I had to stop my tour,
that there was no El Dorado; their vast skies were also ours.

II

He stared at the Pacific – and all his men
Look'd at each other with a wild surmise –
Silent, upon a peak in Darien.

– John Keats

36

The year after I arrived in England, I became a newsboy.
I had to deliver a Latin American newspaper to London's
Latino restaurants, kiosks and salsa clubs: there was no joy
in that enterprise, and I was happy when it was done.
The van driver was a man from Colombia called Juan,
who was very religious, went to the Charismatic Church
and would pray while driving, and me, well I just yawned.
We would start very early until all addresses were checked.
Then one day, while doing our rounds, he parked the camper,
looked at me and said: *Let's pray together. Here. Right now.*
Think of three wishes, and la virgen purísima will deliver.
He closed his eyes and began to pray. I pretended to follow.
Let me stay here in England, and let me be a poet one day.
He started the engine, winked at me, and the van sped away.

37

(from the British Museum)

A musical horn from the mysterious deserts of the Altiplano
A wool rope, with leather attached, made somehow by the Aymara
A plumed arrow from the Amazon that killed a Conquistador
A pottery vessel unearthed at midnight in Atacama
A bolas of three weights bound by a lost Gaucho from the Andes
A figurine made of a shell found by chance in the Gulf of Darien
A knotted armband with toucan feathers from the shores of Vaupés
A stone tool made by a blind Indian boy from Neuquén
A mythic terracotta black 'fire cloud' vessel from Colombia
A man's dancing cloak worn by the witches of Paraguay
A blade and a spear-head found somewhere in Patagonia
A Colonial coin used by sightseers and healers, uncovered in Uruguay
A gold bracelet with motifs of vengeful felines from Nasca
A bronze jaguar figure pulled from a temple ruin in Cuzco

38

When I first met you, I really thought you were Swedish
with your thick black hair, your green eyes, your pale skin,
but you told me you were, in fact, Argentinean and Jewish.
You thought it was amusing, and showed it with a big grin.
Then you told me you were really more of a Londoner,
that you had come with your Argentine family to England
as a four-year-old, just a few months before the winter
of 1982, that you found it rather gloomy arriving on this island.
We exchanged numbers, you told me you had a girlfriend,
and that it'd be nice to meet up sometime, perhaps in Soho.
And I said *yes!* in my strange English as I had to pretend
that all I wanted was your friendship, and I did it, somehow.
Twenty years later, you still laugh about my Swedish gaffe;
you think I'm clueless about types, and you're right, well . . . half.

39

The gated community El Paraíso Verde, *The Green Paradise*,
is being carved out of the fertile reddish earth of Caazapá,
one of Paraguay's poorest regions. A 21st-century paradigm
where the rich and poor live near but are always kept apart.
Its swelling community formed by the Alpine tribe – Germans,
Austrians and Swiss immigrants. They're escaping the palisade
of socialist trends, compulsory vaccinations, the State's hands,
as well as 5G, fluoridated water, and all the healthcare mandates.
They are fleeing from the old matrix, the one-world-order,
now settling in this rural idyll dominated by cattle ranching.
Like Elisabeth F. Nietzsche, the philosopher's zealot sister,
who in 1886 built Nueva Germania, a proto-fascist clearing
in Latin America's heart. Once again, there is an Aryan
colony untouched by Jewish influence, Covid-fenced, agrarian.

40

A year after we first met, I proposed living together, and . . .
you said *why not?* We moved to a tiny flat on Columbia Road.
You'd split up with a girlfriend. I was your first boyfriend.
Both of us Argentineans. The East End became our new abode.
It took us a while to get used to each other. I was impatient,
obsessed with tidying up, ate food you found disgusting.
You were a young artist going out most nights. An ardent
career ahead of you. You told me your art was the first thing.
All I wanted was a home, a new family. Then, an art residency
came for you in Munich. And we thought that's it. Either this
will make or break us. Those winter months away, the hesitancy,
my visits, the long phone calls. The things we began to miss.
And one day, while on Marienplatz, you said, let's not be apart,
and came back to London, and things changed – a new start.

41

As a child, I was obsessed with horror movies, gothic novels,
read all of Stephen King's books, Poe's darkest short stories,
watched the whole Friday the 13th series, loved ghosts, devils
and spirits. I was fascinated by the dark side of Buenos Aires.
Mother had died already. And our house was getting sombre.
At night, I would see apparitions, odd shadows, a procession
of little creatures hiding out behind our back garden's arbour.
I couldn't sleep at night, yet kept feeding my spooky obsession.
That stopped, eventually. But one day, after we moved in together
and you were having a shower, I decided to scare you, hid
behind our bedroom door, placed pillows under the bedcover,
and waited patiently pretending to be in bed, proud of what I did.
When you came out, and I shouted *booo!!*, you howled like a monster
and promised me if I did *that* again, I'd be your *ex*-lover.

42

The Harpy eagle emerges from the rainforest, like a goddess
crisscrossing the vast highlands of South America. She flies
over the woodland borders. A perfect huntress of the forests
with slate-black feathers and the most fulgurous of eyes:
grey, bright red, *alight!* A rare queen, her head crowned
with a double crest, named for that half-human, half-bird
hybrid from Greece, a spirit carrying the dead to a mound
in Hades, snatching souls away, swooping, much feared.
She's soaring away from humans now, the elusive Harpy eagle
of the neotropics, rising from the Mata Atlântica, the Amazon,
clenching with her large talons pin monkeys and electric eels
to feed the hungry gods awaiting her in the clouds at dawn.
And when she ascends above the dwindling jungles,
people think they see that other monster – hungry, insatiable.

43

At a London school with many Latinx students,
I read my poems about gay love, family and exile.
The kids listen with attention, some are fluent
in Spanish, others half-speak, and they smile.
They look at me maybe thinking of their parents
who came here, like me, and live in two languages.
They're curious about my stories, my life in Kent,
how I write and why, my Argentinean baggage.
Then I ask them about their lives, their dreams.
They raise their hands, bursting to tell me
all about their latest ambitions, and their faces beam.
They're eager to share their pride in their families.
A boy points at another: *His father works in Parliament!*
Everyone laughs. *Well . . . as a cleaner, with disinfectant.*

44

Like the dusty Archive of America's First Planetarium,
with its small sundials, rare telescopes and pocket globes,
or the Global Seed Vault, a giant underground aquarium
buried deep on an island between Norway and the North Pole.
Like the gargantuan Museum of Anthropology in Mexico City,
with its Aztec calendar – the Stone of the Sun – and the tomb-
stone and jades of Pakal. Like the Gold Museum of Bogotá City,
packed with necklaces, bracelets and trunks, room after room.
So, my own museum grows every day in this English diaspora,
a collection of objects acquired (who knows) to tell my story;
letters from Argentina, stones, books, photos from a lost camera,
and all the things you gave me as presents, a gay love's allegory.
Sometimes, I wander through those corridors, long and intricate,
looking at my past, my two countries – a diorama for an immigrant.

45

I read in the *Butterflies and Moths in Britain* field guide
that many of this country's species are, in fact, nomadic,
that they move from place to place over the countryside
in search of nourishment, always unwearying, pragmatic.
A primaeval instinct compels them every year to gather,
responding to the sudden season's changes. They follow
the sun's path, the way the North winds blow, some scatter
over oceans and mountains, others look down on seas below.
An impulse urges them to move, they perpetually pursue
the better place to feed, drink and mate till they're dying,
their inner compass always at work to chart their routes
crossing to Spain, the Southern Hemisphere, oh migrating
British butterflies: clouded yellows, swallowtails, painted ladies,
red admirals, the milkweed, the large whites, the fritillaries.

46

You're at work in your studio finishing your drawings of hell
and Baroque paradises for an art exhibition at the Soane.
There are scenes of utter madness; the tallest casino hotel
with a richly polychrome relief showing a Venus mausoleum,
aeronautical crafts of various types plunging to the ground,
a resort where erotic harlequins and a dame are on holiday.
There's also an imposing port, a giant lobster, a drab round-
about and a flyover, even a bright red scene of early artillery.
The work is finished. These mad creations and ornate elements
depict a delirious world I know well, of impossible fantasies
and Rococo excesses, a world of curls, frills, and pediments.
I've seen you carefully conjure each of those bizarre galaxies.
And on one sheet, you drew yourself as a baby in a pram
pushed by your mother down a sinuous Jardín Botánico path.

47

In 1590, the worst plague in South American history struck.
It halted the Jesuits' teaching. Priests withdrew southwest,
down the Ypané River to Paraguay, praying for better luck,
for the good days of conversions at Pope Gregory's request.
But despair set in. Converting the Indians – a hopeless cause.
All Paraguay's Jesuits were summoned to a crisis concilium
in Argentina. There was no future for their saintly exercise
so, according to their superior, a father called Paéz, the teaching
had to be abandoned. It was too risky for the holy reverends
from the order of Loyola, who asked for those 'who strive
to serve as soldiers of Almighty God, to fight for the sole defence
of the faith, and for the progress of souls in Christian life'.
Not a simple decision, Father Paéz tells us, since 'the Jesuits lost
two hundred thousand Indians, all ripe for the kingdom of Christ'.

48

For almost twenty years, you've cut my hair, a rite
You've practised in front of our bathroom mirror,
me half-naked, turning slowly to the left, then right,
looking at my hair on the floor and getting nearer
all around me, as you would tell me to please stop
moving, to stay still as a statue, and I'd comply,
but only for a few seconds, until the tiny hairs atop
my nose would make me move, and I'd be out of line.
I'd always be happy with your monthly cut, whatever
the result, would later shower thinking of you so close,
the way you know my head, my receding lines, never
complaining about the task or how much my hair grows.
There's nothing that gives me more pleasure than you
stroking the top of my head and giving me a new hairdo.

49

Today the oxygen pump arrived and I've wasted no time
in unwrapping the cardboard box, connecting the tubes
to the tiny machine, plugging the thing to the power line,
checking if it worked, if all its parts were ready to use.
I submerged its heavy balls into the stagnated pond,
saw how the goldfish looked suspiciously at first, then
began to swim fast, chasing each other, bubbles beyond
their wildest dreams, breaking the slime. And that's when
I saw father on his deathbed, his oxygen tank just arrived,
me connecting him to it, through the thin tubes that smelt
of salt and chlorine and wet hospitals, while father, deprived
of air, looked at me as I switched the thing on, then left.
And a nurse telling me, once he was connected to it, nourished
by breathing gas, his lungs would rely on the tank, like these fish.

50

A sandy hillside rises in Arica, right on Chile's edge
and the vast Atacama desert, the world's driest place.
The slope is dotted with perfectly cut orange badges,
each for a set of skeletal remains that lies beneath, face-
less, stripped of skin, veins, and organs, all swaddled
in elaborate confections of fine reeds, tough sea lion
skins, alpaca wool, clay, and on top: wigs of mottled
human hair, like helmets. A tourist site for Chileans
to learn about their past. This pre-Columbian ossuary
reminds me of marked plots I once saw in Argentina,
dotted with small flags and numbers, a strange mortuary
under the sun where our history lies, made by hyenas.
Forensic experts and human rights lawyers were searching.
For in those secret fields, many ended up 'disappearing'.

51

In a book about great city plans, I find Buenos Aires
drawn by a French cartographer called Jacques Bellin –
a 1756 map with a few blocks painted as pink as cherries;
one fort, a cathedral, a hospital, the convent of La Merci.
In the middle of it all, an empty square, La Grande Place,
and on its western side, the city hall. Everything so sparse,
a godforsaken place surrounded by the muddy River Plate,
too meagre, impoverished, deficient, not a city but a curse.
You often draw cities, strange maps, metropolises deserted
with no men around. Like in Bellin's map, hardly any trees
but low rickety bushes, weeds and green pastures painted
like scattered insects lost in that faraway place by the sea.
You always say your whimsical cities come from one source:
Buenos Aires, that mythical place you left as a boy of four.

52

A week inside this old house, both in self-isolation,
by the sea, our elderly next-door neighbour passing,
we ask each other, *how do you feel today?* and so on.
We live in a haze, waking up, reading, then napping.
Your mother calls to say she bought us an oximeter.
It rained last night, the sea winds blew over our pots.
How do you feel today? Starlings gather at the feeder,
goldfish suspended in the pond, crystallised red dots.
The wind picks up again, and I suddenly remember
the TV programme we watched last night, on Vermeer
and that ruby spot in the *Girl with Red Hat*'s eye, a rendered
fleck of light, a beryl spark that shone so bright and clear.
Today you coughed a lot, but we're feeling much better.
¿Cómo te sentís? Still quarantined, like Medieval lepers.

53

In *The Witch*, they begin to levitate around the bonfire
while she, the Argentine actress, sees those women lifting
their bare arms, legs, breasts above the towering pyre.
They laugh, shriek and rise up, the cold night shifting
into something else. We have witches here, too, that turn
to night owls, stall vendors, foragers, they also cackle
when the sea tides turn and the moon grows, they burn
incense in their Deal cottages, offer their reddest apples
to the unaware. Once, I went with mother to a local witch
to try to cure her of her leukaemia, to stop the poison
from running through her veins. The old curandera reached
for her rosary and said odd prayers like the strangest nun.
Mother later said she didn't believe in necromancers,
¡pero que las hay, las hay! she'd declare – never say never.

54

From the wetlands of the Pantanal at dusk, a toucan ascends
to the tallest palm tree in the clearance. There, it measures
the pink sky, macaws that begin to roost; she extends
her glossy black wings as if sizing all things with feathers.
Her immense orange beak opens in a perfect V-shape, a sign
before the light is gone, and she, too, is forced to retreat
to the forest's heart, or perhaps beyond, to that all-divine
place where she'll shift into another being and be complete.
Like the Nagual, that human being that can shapeshift,
turning all at once into their tonal animal counterpart,
morphing into a golden bird, a snake, a fireball – such gifts
to the Natural world of the Aztecs, masters of that rare art.
So when the toucan vanishes from the thicket at twilight,
people say she's no longer there, but her spirit in flight.

55

Three days before father died, a rare butterfly
appeared in his room. It was huge, bright blue
and yellow. My father was half-conscious, dry
as a leaf. I touched the dusty wing, and it flew
fast towards him. *¡Papá, mirá! ¡Una mariposa azul!*
He tried to smile, let it reach his stained pillow,
he said it was surely a sign, an omen. I, on a stool
by his deathbed. Then, the big butterfly glowed,
a lapis lazuli stone in a house in Buenos Aires,
the bedroom turned cobalt, an underwater world
where the two of us were floating, the azure fairies
in a children's book. Everything was blue, pearled
with the flapping of dark wings. It all faded in seconds.
The realisation of his falling, like in the tale of Icarus.

56

(South American butterflies)

Eurytides columbus, Morpho achillaena,
Eresia anieta, Stalachis phlegia,
Catagramma cynosura, Ageronia velutina,
Eurytides dolicaon, Colias lesbia,
Papilio homothoas, Agrias sardanapalus,
Papilio menatius, Eresia simois,
Papilio androgeus, Catoblepia berecynthus,
Papilio himeros, Heliconius phyllis,
Lemonias zygia, Battus belus,
Leucochimona icare, Papilio neyi,
Livendula aminias, Battus ingenuus,
Argyrogrammana occidentalis, Callithea hewitsoni,
Mesene bomilcar, Euselasia cuprea,
Ancyluris rubrofilum, Heliconius narcaea.

57

In our very first car, driving on an empty country lane
one sunny Friday morning in May, with a light zephyr
blowing from the southwest, thinking of Joan Fontaine
in that *Rebecca* scene where she looks at Laurence Olivier
as he drives and both smile under the sun and are content.
We're driving to have lunch together by a tiny Kentish bay,
our first road trip, and you're at the wheel! We invent
our own film. You say twice today it'll be a perfect day.
And to think that father always thought I should drive,
that for him a real man should love his car. Yet I refused
to be his ideal son, the only one he had, choosing to live
a life abroad. The prodigal son he, at first, disapproved of.
Thank God you learnt to drive, and not me, I said to you,
as we sped towards the English sea, rough and blue.

58

While clearing out papers before we leave this beach house,
I find, hidden among old letters, postcards and utility bills,
a few photos of our trip together to China, not yet spouses
but our first journey as boyfriends, fresh from it all, thrilled.
In one, we're embracing outside the Temple of Heaven.
I'm leaning against one of its carmine doors, you look straight
at the camera, wearing a striped shirt and a pair of blue jeans.
In another, we're on a local bus smiling like on a first date.
At dinner, we talk about what to do with all these memories,
if it's worth holding on to photos and papers, if by doing so
we kill what we've lived and seen, going back to a repository
of the mind, if it's not better to live in a present that flows.
We finished packing over the weekend, ready for transport,
capsules with messages to our future, time machines of sorts.

59

As I unpack my library and everything inside,
the long-forgotten books, Spanish language novels,
the left-out drafts of unfinished poems, guides
to birds and English trees, I pause to look at a fossil
perched on a shelf. A stone we found on a Deal beach,
a tiny pebble that, on closer inspection, hides within
the perfect outline of two prehistoric leaves, each
caught in that precise moment, preserved in flint.
Like this ancient sea house we're about to leave,
an old inn you lovingly restored. I watched you
peel off its layers, strip back its floors, relieved
to find, beneath its recent story, some ageing clues.
Two leaves, a fossil, the years by the English Channel,
bits from our life's chronology, an archive dismantled.

60

Nobody had seen the Tequila fish swim upstream
in the Teuchitlán River in Jalisco, it was extinct
apparently, after more invasive and exotic bream
conquered that creek, a disappearance linked
to water pollution. The *Zoogoneticus tequila* died
forever, with its celeste speckles, yellow-hued tail,
named after the volcano looming north of its site,
now inactive but mostly crowned with agave trails.
Yet thanks to conservationists from the Chester Zoo,
the 'charismatic little fish' has returned to its home,
and it's now thriving and breeding too, who knew
it could be revived, unlike the stumptooth minnow.
People bathe in the blue river when the heat strikes
as the Tequila fish dart around, back from the afterlife.

61

Today, I went for my weekly swim in the London Fields Lido.
The November day was grey and cold, and it began to drizzle.
I quickly undressed in the changing room, put on my speedos,
left my bag in the locker before I stepped outside. I shrivelled
half-naked as the steam rose from the pool to the bare Planes,
also defenceless, shaken on that unholy day – el Día de los Muertos.
Hardly anyone in the water: an old man with a golden chain,
the lifesaver in a woolly coat, high up in his chair like a scarecrow.
That's when I saw the bony back of a woman and thought of Mother;
how, despite her losing weight by the day, she kept going,
not knowing that through her blood ran a poison like no other,
leaving purple anemones as she bruised her skin, *those things* growing.
And to think that Father and the Doctor decided not to tell her,
to somehow make her life easier, delaying that nightmare.

62

I read that on his voyage chasing to find the Northwest Passage,
he began to drown in an interior deluge. He was a wreck,
sank into a black mood, lost touch with reality and punished
his crew at the slightest whim. Cook paced the ship's deck
and flew into rages that the seamen onboard called *tōeres,*
after a Tahitian stomping dance. He spread the worst of terrors
across the islands, torched entire villages, carved big crosses
into natives' flesh in revenge for petty crimes. '*God's measures*.'
Even before he became a god, the explorer's true act of divinity
was violence of the erratic kind. As supplies began to run low,
his ship, the HMS Resolution, sighted a paradise of tranquillity.
Rather than landing, he insisted that they keep sailing and go
interminably around the coast. The unhinged captain circled
the island as the year 1779 began. Eyes from the beach curdled.

63

Looking at the tulips explode in the garden, feathery
like Josephine Baker's dancing skirts, how they expand
after the rain, remembering you brought them for me
one Sunday from a shop by the Deal station newsstand
and told me: *Plant them soon, get our garden multicoloured*
after the long grey winter. Outside, all clay pots were bare
until that morning when the first green just unfolded
and I rushed to tell you of its appearance, and we stared
at them. Like the first time I grew my own tulip, a present
brought on a plane from the Southern Andes, the long wait
for weeks until the speckled full cup appeared, a scent-
less totem I worshipped like my own God as a boy of eight,
enacting from memory the story of Jack and the Beanstalk,
as tiny shoot quickly grew to a marbled castle atop a rope.

64

Xul Solar works all day in his simple, prismic house
north of Buenos Aires. The deserted city, a gleaming oven.
His place in the Delta Tigre stands on tall, white posts,
it overlooks a meandering river baked by the midday sun.
They called him the astrologer of the pampas, a translator
of worlds only he knows. On his studio walls, floating cities
drawn in primary colours, a cosmos south of the equator,
multiple towers and ladders, mounds with childlike faces.
He's ready for *Pan ajedrez*, a chess game he devised abroad.
Most of the pieces marked with a consonant or a symbol,
some stamped with numbers. On the checkered board,
squares painted with a combination of red & black vowels.
Borges arrives. They play together, each moves a pawn
and as the warm Argentinean night falls, new words form.

65

After my breakfast alone while you were still asleep,
I read Goethe's *Italian Journey* in this quiet Roman garden
by the Orto Botanico and the Basilica, how he keeps
writing about soon leaving Rome before visiting again
the Colosseum on a full-moon night as if he'd want to say
something else by that eerie light bathing the ancient city,
looking at the ruins and broken statues of the Appian Way,
that even at night, he could see it all clearly and still get dizzy.
We're also leaving Rome tomorrow night, reluctantly
after spending here a secret long weekend honeymoon
walking by the Tiber, lying naked in the Hotel Villa Riari,
looking at how the stone pines gleamed under a giant moon,
remembering the first time we came here as young lads on a date
and you filmed all of Borromini's churches with a 1975 Super-8.

66

In *The Voyage Out*, Rachel Vinrace travels to South America on her father's cruise ship for a long and auspicious voyage. The ship is full of characters – snobbish Latin Americans, Russians and English passengers with Victorian heritage. There's Clarissa Dalloway making her grand appearance, the bookish St John Hirst, and also the arty Helen Ambrose, all going south, to an unknown place with sun in abundance, some are on a journey of self-discovery, to escape their woes. On board, all sorts of satiric interactions occur – the English leave behind corseted England, and they're slowly changing into louder, more colourful players. The pomp relinquished. At night, the air turns hotter and heavier, as do the evenings. Before the novel's end, though, what's being sought is never found as Rachel Vinrace, our main protagonist, dies of fever.

67

The fossilist W. J. Holland in *To the River Plate and Back*
writes about seeing the imposing city of Buenos Aires,
how its cranes and buildings rise up from the busy deck
of the *Vasari* and quotes the poet Wordsworth: 'Ships, towers,
domes, theatres, and temples lie, / Open unto the fields . . . All bright
and glittering in the smokeless air.' Then, he visits the aviary
in the Zoo, is amazed by the largest raptorial bird in flight;
the condor with its great wings, a beast 'imposing and scary.'
And when setting up a replica of the northern Diplodocus
at the National Museum, he spends days and nights piecing
all the bones, putting the bits together as his Magnum Opus
to the city. He's elated when the sauropod starts pointing
in the right direction. A large neck, a whip-like tail, a mouth
with a toothy jaw open in readiness to swallow the South.

68

In the emptiness of this house, a husk amongst debris
left behind after the removal vans left. A stark marking
on the bedroom wall where the cupboard used to be,
holes with nails, useless without the framed paintings.
No chairs, no sofa, all the carpets gone, the tables
left with their four legs, running through Middle Street
towards Dover and the A2 motorway. Old lamp cables
twisting along the dusty skirting board. We then retreat
to the hollowed living room and sit on the bare floor.
It reminds me of when we first moved here, you suddenly say,
and I travel back to those years, standing at the Deal shore,
looking at the lights in Belgium, France, not too far away.
How this seaside place, this house, was like a promise
of eonian love and companionship, a pelagic nest for us.

III

From the traveller we have
the senseless geography
the chance of flight

– Cristina Peri Rossi

69

Charles Darwin spent over eight months around Patagonia,
and wrote about it, describing it only in negative terms:
without habitation, water or trees, unlike the lush Amazonia,
barely able to support a few plants, not many passeriformes.
He travelled on the Beagle from where he wrote his journal
about an immense land of mysterious creatures, the eeriest place
where 'the hour of life has run its course' and become infernal.
A land 'where Death and Decay prevail'. A grotesque case.
The 22-year-old naturalist kept detailed accounts of his journey
to the end of the world, the antipode of a verdant England,
how different that barren place was from his birth country,
bearing 'the stamp of having lasted for ages', a vast wasteland.
And from that Southern plainness grew a new kind of theory,
as he pondered why those wastes had taken hold of his memory.

70

The only board game we ever had here was Monopoly.
I bought it to pass the time when we first moved to Deal.
We played it a few times and soon got bored. Honestly,
it's just going around in circles buying houses or avoiding jail.
In Argentina, we played with the local version, the Estanciero,
the cattle farmer, trying to buy ranches, animals, properties,
fancy flats in Buenos Aires, ending up with no money. Zero!
A game to learn about adulthood, mortgages and poverty.
You live like teenagers, my sister often tells us. No children
or attachments, like true bohemians. Our house is a fantasy
castle filled with many ornaments, a strange Baroque pavilion
where one man draws, and the other composes elegies.
And in your studio, an old chess game of bright red pieces
we never played with. Just for effect, a folly, small caprices.

71

Once, we went with Pablo to the small subtropical island
of Ilha Grande and saw howler monkeys, giant spiders,
red crabs the size of trucks returning from the scrubland.
A honeymoon of sorts as we swam in the greenest rivers
and clearest seas of South America. The coastal reaches
of a mystical land of plenty, the perpetual hovering
of iraí bees over our breakfast table, the endless beaches
of a Brazil of the imagination – lush, vibrant, bustling.
Yet the Mata Atlântica was vanishing behind the shacks
of Angra dos Reis, while the local boys played football
in front of makeshift hostels lining up the dusty tracks.
In Paraty, we saw the square, the old port, from where all
the gold of Minas Gerais, Goiás and Mato Grosso was sent
north, to make grey European churches more resplendent.

72

When Humboldt travelled to South America on a whim
he wrote that he was never tired of admiring the charms
of the southern sky, that an unknown feeling awoke in him
when crossing from one hemisphere to another, the stars
he had known since infancy beginning to vanish in the sky.
He also wrote that when he caught sight of a low-lying island,
he didn't see any signs of life through the telescope, only cacti
in the form of strange candelabra, and large mounds of sand.
And as he was about to go ashore, he saw two pirogues sailing
along the coast, and in each, eighteen Guaiquerí Indians naked
to the waist. He thought they looked so muscular, compelling,
with a skin colour between shining brown and coppery red.
He felt aroused and later wrote: 'Nothing excites a discoverer more
than the sublime and magnificent nature he is about to explore.'

73

A new addition (Pablo's gift) to my cabinet of curiosities –
the Crookes radiometer, also known as the light mill.
It is an airtight glass bulb with some intriguing qualities:
it measures electromagnetic radiation intensity with a whirl
of its metal vanes as they rotate on a spindle when exposed
to sunlight entering my writing studio in Deal. It answers
with a faster spin as light intensifies, otherwise it slows.
It was invented by Sir William Crookes, a Victorian pioneer
who, after the great success of his glass bulb results
changed the whole of chemistry and physics, decided
to turn to spiritualism and the study of the occult,
to try to detect previously undetected forces, and he did.
He managed to speak with his brother in Central America
who had died laying a telegraph cable from Cuba to Florida.

74

A long-nose male harlequin frog (*Atelopus longirostrex*)
whistles in the cloud forests of Ecuador's tropical Andes.
Its brown skin with large yellow spots is a cosmic vortex
to attract its near orbiting mate like Saturn to his Tethys.
It keeps still on a mossy rock by a stream, then climbs
to the highest point, a summit, for all dwellers to hear.
Nearby, a group of brown-faced spider monkeys mime
each other while a Chocó toucan sings, then disappears.
The small frog with its pronounced snout calls and calls,
its throat expands, warming the mist clouds that descend
as the place is shrouded in water drops before night falls,
turning the Amazonian forest into a loud choral blend.
I once heard his strange call as a teenager as it got silent.
A song pierced the forest like a foreign tongue, defiant.

75

At lunch, we talked at length about family –
how everything seems to be disintegrating,
how being migrants made our forebears weary
of solitude, abandonment, how by recreating
a nation at home, they kept their memories portable,
how they began a new life in distant Buenos Aires.
We talked about our life in England, a plausible
family of two men facing each other for years.
At some point, we thought of distant relatives,
cousins, aunts, great-uncles, some now dead,
the tree binding us to a place, the long genitive
branches of our own blood, the severed threads.
It all began with the dream I tried to decipher
of a large house, and inside – a fire, no survivors.

76

When Darwin first arrived in Tierra del Fuego, *fire's land*,
after finishing travelling through Patagonia, he kept close
to the Fuegian shore, followed the inhospitable ground
of the Staten lands visible to him amidst the clouds.
The sea was dark blue, almost black, and the crew
quickly thought it a bad omen, their worst talisman
foretelling the future could soon be dark, a dreary clue
that the biologist dismissed at once, such empirical man.
At noon, the *Beagle* anchored in the Bay of Good Success,
and was saluted 'in a manner becoming the inhabitants
of this savage land'. A group of Fuegians, partly undressed
and concealed by the forest, waved at them in a religious trance.
'The savages followed the ship, and just before dark, we saw their fire
and again heard their wild cry', he wrote later, recalling the pyres.

77

We sometimes imagine moving out elsewhere
to start anew in a faraway country. We toy with Italy
for its churches, its statues, its beautiful marble squares,
the food and ancient cities. We think of starting in Sicily
and from there going to Egypt, to live near the river Nile,
or to Greece, to escape to a town under a foreign sun.
You making drawings, me writing books, both in exile,
fleeing the London life as ogre fugitives, two men on the run.
Like the mighty Creature in Mary Shelley's *Frankenstein*,
who swears revenge against humans, slays his maker's
friends, and then demands he creates a new companion
like himself – another outcast – a pariah – for solace and laughter.
And says if he agrees, no human being will ever see them again,
fleeing 'to the vast wilds of South America', that unimaginable terrain.

78

(Native peoples of Argentina)

Pilagá, Mapuche,
Tilián, Quechua, Sanavirón,
Chané, Iogys, Qom (Toba), Tehuelche,
Chicha, Kolla Atamaqueño, Comechingón,
Charrúa, Ranquel, Chorote, Wichí, Lule, Chulupí,
Huarpes, Lule Vilela, Selk'Nam (Onas), Tapiete,
Tonokoté,Tastil, Diaguita, Corundí,
Atacama, Guaycurú, Tonokoté,
Omaguaca, Fiscara,
Mbyá Guaraní,
Toara,
Moqoit (Mocoví),
Kolla,
Ocloya.

79

(A Latin American Photographic spread, The Guardian*)*

A dancing clown in a Coatepec street, Veracruz, Mexico.
Boys wearing masks juggling tennis balls at a traffic light
in Barra da Tijuca, Brazil. Two girls from Puerto Rico
swimming in a pool in San Juan, the sky pink and bright.
A vegetable seller with a red hat napping at her stand
somewhere in Lima, Peru, after working all night long.
A Santera girl crying by a mass grave, her clasped hands
as a relative is buried in Carabobo, Venezuela. Strong
men from the local community of San Rafael, Veracruz,
forming a line with sombreros in their gnarled hands,
to offer wildflowers at the burial of Rafaela Sánchez.
A girl killed by her boyfriend for refusing his demands.
An officer in riot gear amid smoke bombs charging furiously
at bare-chested protesters in Plaza Dignidad, Santiago, Chile.

80

We were going to be late for our clandestine civil partnership
at Tower Hamlets Registry Office on 236 Cable Street.
We couldn't find a taxi (not one) to take us there – the first blip! –
so we jumped into a bus and sat nervously in the front seats.
Ellis, our best man, was already standing in the waiting room
with a homemade picnic box and a bottle of frappé Prosecco.
Catherine arrived with a signed card that said, *Happy Grooms!*
A Syrian couple whispered next to her; both were from Aleppo.
Then, the four of us were led to a little white station
at the back of the old building, with a small sofa and a desk
with a sign that warned against making false declarations
or else . . . *Perjury!* The whole thing was rather picturesque.
At our impromptu picnic by Hawksmoor's St George-in-the-East,
Ellis pulled the party poppers. We found glitter for days after the feast.

81

I see the *Battle of Curupayty* painting by Cándido López,
where Argentine troops begin to attack the Paraguayans.
There are dead soldiers everywhere, cannon shells
exploding in the deadliest war between Latin Americans.
A combat rages on the battlefield with much violence
to finally kill General Díaz, Paraguay's headstrong ruler,
wiping out half its people for their treacherous arrogance.
For some, Britain was somehow involved in the warfare
of Curupayty, pulling the strings behind the curtains,
plotting to flood Paraguay's surging economy with Albion's
goods, to plant cotton for Lancashire mills in its fertile terrain.
Others thought the calamity's causes lay solely within the region.
In the naive-style large painting, all I see is utter carnage,
nameless corpses in swamps, smoke rising – death's full rage.

82

You've begun a new ink drawing for an art commission
and I can hear you stretching the paper over a board,
watering it to make it smooth for the line's definitions,
waiting for the paper to dry while searching on the floor
for the right books to give you inspiration. I follow you
from next door – my writing studio – as you cross your room,
begin to prepare your pots of water, rulers, the ink brews
you will use before drawing with pencils, consumed
by an idea or two: a Baroque garniture, a Rococo artefact.
Sometimes, I'll enter your studio, and you'll ask me
what I think, if I enjoy the composition and if it's exact,
if I agree with the overall design and like what I see.
If I praise your shapes and lines in your drawing, you smile,
but when I disagree, you often complain . . . *then* later comply.

83

'December 6th, 1833. The *Beagle* sailed from the River Plate,
never again to enter its muddy stream.' Charles Darwin wrote
a few observations at dusk while at sea as the intense heat abated,
and all he could hear were the local cicadas, even from his boat.
'Several times when the ship has been some miles off the mouth
of the Plata, and at other times when off the shores of Patagonia,
we have been surrounded by insects.' He heard of a severe drought
in Argentina, of the infernal winds blowing from the Amazonia.
So one evening, when the *Beagle* was off the Bay of San Blas,
vast numbers of flying bugs covered the ship like a strange mantle
from the underworld, 'in bands or flocks of countless myriads,
extended as far as the eye could range'. Darwin was startled
and heard crew members shout while pointing at the sky.
The English seamen were yelling, *It's snowing butterflies!*

84

We're returning from Argentina after our January break,
an energising trip after seeing all the family again;
my sister, a writer living in a gated community with a lake,
an elderly aunt, and a younger sister who never complains.
It's high Summer. We spent weeks in swimming pools,
trying to avoid the midday heat under verandas, cooling off,
enjoying this oasis in the middle of the British winter, that cruel
darkness awaiting us. Going back home is always a trade-off.
Then, on the plane, we remember everything we've done – meals
that never end, trips to see distant relatives comparing both
countries, how bad things are there and how better here, an ideal
place to visit, then leave. A nation with so much except growth.
Until the plane begins its descent, and after weeks with the sun out,
we enter layers of thick fog, the little light colliding with clouds.

The Crown of the Kings

I said that's *home* there, as the ferry veered and the wind hummed.
Looking out from our house's window with my binoculars,
I imagined being on that ship crossing the Channel, succumbing
to the rugged English coast. Or suddenly transformed to an astrologer
following the Southern star in that other dark sea, incandescent.
I often use spyglasses to see the roofs of neighbouring houses,
the way people live here, what's on their TVs, their fluorescent
fish tanks glowing in the dark, clotheslines, hanging trousers.
Pablo brought me these binoculars many years ago on an outing
to a nature reserve in Norfolk, where all I wanted to do was see
the local birds, the butterflies, to put a name to these new things,
to discover this English realm together; we two young *argies*.
Beyond these lenses, there is another world still awaiting us,
a place I often imagine traversing together with a field glass.

'*A place I often imagine traversing together with a field glass*',
Darwin tells the Gaucho as he is about to cross a land south
of Buenos Aires, both galloping, he's on a horse called *Grass*,
Pasto. It's August 1833, and his *Beagle* arrived off the mouth
of the Río Negro, where he disembarked. They're travelling
north to Bahía Blanca. He takes his binoculars and inspects
the land, then makes some notes in a tiny notebook, scribbling
a few words: 'Everywhere the landscape wears the same aspect;
a dry gravelly soil supports tufts of brown withered grass, and
low scattered bushes, armed with thorns'. Sighs. Shortly after,
they see a famous tree surrounded by rocks and coarse sand.
The Gaucho tells him that the Indians revere it as the altar
of Walleechu. The tree has no leaves. In their place, a splendid
sight: threads with offerings. Cigars, bread, cascabels suspended.

A sight! Threads with offerings, cigars, bread, cascabels suspended
from the Ekeko figurine. *It'll bring you good luck. And plenty of money!*
the Bolivian woman tells me. The Coya doll dream is open-ended.
It also has little dollar bills, beans and coca leaves. A tiny dummy
I find irresistible. She tells me it's the Tiwanakan god of abundance,
embodying prosperity in the mythology of the Bolivian Altiplano.
I'm in La Paz, travelling alone tasting for the first time independence
as I discover Latin America, its forests, cathedrals, ruins and volcanos.
I buy the Ekeko at the market, put it in my rucksack, rub his cheeks
for my auspicious journey. Decades later, in my house in England,
I place the paper maché figurine over my studio bookcase, a trick
to bring me good luck while reminding me of that faraway land.
In its gaping, smiling mouth, there is a hole to put a slim cigarette
for his own pleasure, to make the little man into a good amulet.

For his pleasure, to make the little man into a good amulet,
the English explorer gives him a telescope and orders him to look
for an island. The tall sailor brought him good luck and is adamant
the story will repeat. The *Beagle* sailed from Valparaíso, and it took
days to survey Southern Chile to the broken land of the Chonos,
a fine Archipelago. On November 10th, 1834, the sailor points to a dot
in the Pacific. '*Land ahoy!*' shouts the seaman on deck as Darwin notes
in his diary the arrival to Chiloé, the greenest Eden, 'a beautiful spot.'
Days later, the sailor looks through his telescope and sees smoke rising
from the volcano of Osorno, a highland formed like a perfect cone,
white with snow, standing out in front of the Cordillera, billowing
steam from the summit. South American terns, wrens and cocoi herons
call to the gods to appease the giant. A condor flies above the mountain.
'To live on this island is a rare miracle; everything thrives like a fountain.'

They live off this island. As if money flows like a fountain.
That's why so many people want to come here, our neighbour in Deal
told us. He's seen it on TV. They cross the Channel on bogus claims
and overstay before bringing all their dependents. *It is unreal!*
He said Great Britain is broken; nothing is like it used to be.
He's retired now and collects old nautical instruments – maps,
compasses, astrolabes, telescopes and spheres to chart the seas.
He knows we're both migrants from Argentina, but perhaps
he forgot. Pablo speaks with a north London accent. I'm obviously not
from here. As we walked back home that night, we looked at each other,
somehow puzzled, picturing him in that house, his political thoughts,
how he showed us his antique collection like a zealous grandmother.
There was a full moon, and it was making the beach shine bronze.
We could clearly see the glowing coast of France, how close it was.

'We could clearly see the glowing coast of France, how close it was',
Darwin writes as he at last departs from England, illusioned
with the many wonders awaiting him in South America, the course
his life is taking, what he's about to discover, his theory of evolution.
The big ship is leaving, and suddenly, his youth is left behind:
he is a young man of 22, ready to write his pioneering masterpiece.
During the trip, he has many nightmares about a chieftain confined
to his country. His mother appears, yet he knows she's long deceased.
At some point in the long voyage, he begins to feel unease, sweats
most days, thinks he has already caught an illness and will be unable
to start his once-in-a-lifetime trip. The *Beagle* whispers. He regrets
his constant fears, his sudden indecision he deplores as damnable,
imagining eventually returning with his findings to his homeland,
crossing the English Channel on a packed boat back to England.

Crossing the English Channel on a packed boat back to England,
we talked about our Summer trip to the Continent, how familiar
the Mediterranean life seems to us, the way people move their hands,
or talk loudly like Argentineans, the many links there are, how similar.
At first, the sea was calm and blue, and we could see the white froth
trailing behind our ship: a few seagulls followed us on our way home,
perhaps begging for a piece of bread or chips, waving like a tablecloth.
Some passengers were half-asleep, children running like crazy gnomes.
Then the sea got rougher, and the ferry swerved this way and that.
We got closer to our seats, still thinking of those Italian towns, the sea
where we swam like fish, and then France, the food, the sun, the cats
of Menton and Cap Martin, esplanades lined with sylphic palm trees.
Until we saw the white cliffs of Dover, and you pointed straight at them,
and said that's *home* out there, as the ferry veered and the wind hummed.

86

I walked inside the engraving by Joaquín Torres García
América invertida, where South America has turned around,
an ill-shaped supercontinent reshaped like a jumbled Pangaea,
where the Andes face West, and I'm sitting upside down.
A frigate takes me to a reversed Uruguay against the breeze,
a big sun rises in the Pacific, no less, and a moon has six stars!
The Equator has moved South, and the Isthmus is squeezed
like a venomous yarará. América plays like an inverted guitar.
I hear pre-Columbian songs from a distorted instrument,
backward chants to run away from the North. I see a Tiwanaku
rising sideways. The outline of my continent is an experiment
of liberation, a reversed cosmology, a laboratory of the new.
There, a streamlined manifesto for a South American youth.
His ink-on-paper drawing of 1943. 'Our North is the South.'

87

The Purple Land That England Lost, how that refined Victorian expatriate's South American pseudo-fantasy recounts the union of an Englishman with an Argentine before traversing the turbid River Plate to wild Uruguay. There, he ends up fighting the bloodiest of gaucho wars, betraying his wife with local women of ill repute. An oracle of a book – Blood, revolutions, independence, the late years of a tumultuous 19th Century. W. H. Hudson's hysterical allegory of civilisation and barbarism. This was a despatch to his dear England. The obsessive emigré ornithologist recalling the wild pampas, the estancias, the vast green patch speckled with horses, wild Indians and cattle. The naturalist filling the action with high drama. The poet Borges agrees, comparing its 'primitive' strength to Homer's *Odyssey*.

88

After months of writing sonnets, I stop to search for one
about Pablo and me having a little row in our house by the sea.
In that sonnet, I try to convey a sense of ill-temper, how stunned
I am by my own outburst, how his mood darkens: *Don't lie to me!*
You lost my 17th-Century Chinese vase, the small one with a lid. I make
him say that in my poem. And somehow reveal my other sins.
The mood is tense. But then, all is forgiven, and we go back
to having tea in the garden, talking about mundane things.
The search bar doesn't seem to work. The sonnet is gone.
Did I really write about that row? What exactly did I unveil?
He often helped me edit poems. Did he delete it and go on
to finish a large drawing waiting for him in his studio in Deal?
In any case, I often end up losing things; it's in my nature.
Maybe I didn't write it after all, or it's lost, like his Ming garniture.

89

While waiting for the *Beagle* in the estuary of Bahía Blanca
Darwin saw three hundred men sailing down the river
under the command of one Commandant Luis Miranda.
They were mostly 'tame Indians' and yet he quivered.
The Indians passed the night there 'and it was impossible'
he wrote, 'to conceive any thing more wild or more savage
than the scene of the bivouac', a camp for the damnable.
'Some drunk until intoxicated, others just scavenged
the steaming blood of the cattle being slaughtered
for their suppers,' Darwin wrote in his notes for *The Voyage
of the Beagle*, 'then sick from drunkenness, and fuddled,
they cast it up again, were besmeared with filth and carnage.'
How great is the 'difference between savage & civilised man –
It is greater than between a wild & domesticated animal.'

90

In the humid highlands of Mesoamerica, the Quetzal calls
resplendent in opaline greens, her bright red belly ablaze
even under the rain. A solitary pilco hides under waterfalls;
turning into a multicoloured gem on hot, humid days
when all she does is feed on fruits and the tiniest frogs.
A 1733 pair of Quetzal figurines of hard-paste porcelain
sits in a case at the Metropolitan Museum in New York,
their extended wings in an embrace. They sing or are in pain;
we'll never know. Their colours are all wrong: light yellow
where the red should be, muted purple instead of green.
They're about to take flight but are caught in time; an echo
of the Aztec or Mayan cries, frozen in a strange scene.
Emperors from Tenochtitlan wore their feathers in headbands
thinking of the dazzling bird, alone in the deepest woodland.

91

While you were installing the artwork for your retrospective
at the Centre for Contemporary Art in Geneva, I wandered
through the old city, climbed up St-Pierre's stairs for the perspective:
there I saw the spouting Jet d'Eau and the lake, meandered
from the Pont du Mont-Blanc to the ancient cemetery of the Kings
at Plainpalais to see the grave of Borges, and from there, I went
to the Beau Rivage Hotel, where they put us in the best wing
to honour you and your work before the big opening event.
That evening, I was the first to arrive at the museum, and I saw
your drawings, installations, the art videos and suddenly felt
all those years coming back. I could remember when you drew
each piece, where I was then, what you said, the moods, the smells.
And as I walked through the rooms, I could see the whole endeavour:
each day that passes, the hidden thread that binds us together.

92

Humboldt and Bonpland at the Chimborazo Base
and behind them, the highest mountain of Ecuador
rising up, all covered in snow like a tall dessert ice.
All around them, cacti sprouting from a sandy floor.
In the oil painting, natives are building a small fire,
some bring wood, another saddles a mule, one points
at the two European explorers and their weird attire,
while waiting for instructions on how to build a tent.
Then a Quechua presents Humboldt with a telescope
as Bonpland catalogues a plant and a dead condor,
there's also a dog overseeing the scene in the hope
of a bone. A furious tropical rainstorm begins to pour.
Who discovers who, where, what, and in which order,
the puzzled dog ponders, as it looks at the pale explorers.

93

During Charles Darwin's visit to Buenos Aires' biggest corrales, where animals were kept for slaughter to supply food to the beef-eating locals, the young English scientist is amazed by the scale of such a spectacle. He describes how the gaucho, the main chief of the action, uses his lazo to grab all the beasts by their horns, and how he, atop a big horse, can drag them anywhere he chooses, almost breaking their necks. He's enthralled by the twists and turns of the agile cowboy, how when the bullock is conquered and loses the battle, the matador cuts its hamstrings with great care. Then, the scene gets bloodier. He hears the frightful sound of death, a noise more expressive than any he has known among animals or men. He's certain the struggle is at its end. The beast is a gaucho's toy. 'The whole sight is horrible & revolting, the ground is made of bones, while the horses and riders end up completely drenched with gore'.

94

Late in 1981, on a bus from Buenos Aires to São Paulo,
the gay activist Néstor Perlongher writes a long poem
about the Argentine dictatorship, *Corpses* – a slow
decaying string of slaughtered bodies as an omen.
The rotting memories of death, a myriad of places
touched by political violence. An endless journey
through the Serra Geral range, the Araucaria forests
in the cool of the night and also in the early morning.
He crosses the wide Uruguay river, the Iberá morass,
and keeps writing all day long in a Neo-Baroque frenzy.
He thinks of torsos, the profanity of sensual sordidness,
of the well-hidden bodies falling into a turbid sea.
The feverish poem grows, its dark polyvocal sources,
and a recurrent refrain: *They're corpses. They're corpses.*

95

A lorry crosses from Nuevo Laredo in Mexico to Texas.
Outside, the dry land is covered in feather grasses, honey
mesquites and spiny nopales. The heat is infectious.
Encinal appears at a distance, a small town of low dwellings.
On the flat Monarch Highway, trucks race to San Antonio,
an old Chevrolet plays Elvis, a newly wedded couple drives
a brand new caravan to a local motel called Los Demonios.
Above, a red hawk clutches its prey: a few voles, hardly alive.
Then, after passing Von Ormy, he decides to take a detour,
the sun is setting, and the city's bright lights glimmer red,
orange, brown. He smells the land – dirt, oil, sweat, manure.
Someone is shouting. High-pitched voices, muffled.
A day later, the bodies are found: Mexicans – many dozens,
Guatemalans – seven, and piled together – a group of Hondurans.

96

In *The Twilight Zone* by Chilean author Nona Fernández,
a moustached member of the secret police in Chile
walks into the office of a dissident magazine and says
to a reporter he wants to tell a story, to give his testimony.
'The Man Who Tortured People' takes the female journalist
on a strange journey, to the underworld of Pinochet's years,
to the sinister places where young people ceased to exist,
and were dumped into rivers, deserts or sea. They disappeared,
entered into that strange twilight place, like in the TV series
where you can stop time or change identities or travel back
to see faces history can't reach. A rare portal, nebulous, eerie,
to reimagine the dark past of a country, memories in black.
Beyond the known world, there is always another grey zone
(a voiceover); sometimes you cross it, and then you're gone.

97

On a road trip from Bariloche to Villa La Angostura,
returning from spending time with your distant cousin,
we looked at the mountains in the distance, a caesura
during our long conversation. The big Patagonian sun
was sinking, a few deer were grazing by the Andes,
and our taxi driver was telling us of an old local story
about a puma that roamed the highlands, leaving antlers
as leftovers for hunters. That blue peak, a rare allegory.
The road was long and empty, we could see the lake,
the Araucarias carpeting its shores, the radio was on
and it was playing a Mapuche song with a trutruka.
Suddenly the light left us, and we could see Orion.
That night we thought of the solitary feline up there
in the mountains, its glowing eyes, the deer's despair.

98

Every Día de San Valentín, a man would knock at our door,
and bring a big bouquet of red roses to mother with a note:
Te amo, tu Raúl. Mother would place the flowers over a drawer
thinking all day of father at work, the little message he wrote.
And every year, the same ritual. The delivery man, the roses,
the same note, the vase placed in the house like an amulet,
what those flowers meant for her, what the envelope enclosed.
Until she was too ill to walk and was taken away in an ambulance.
And now, every Valentine's Day, I, too, get my own flowers
from you. When I wake up, there is always a homemade card
placed over my desk, a card where you write about us, our
life together, and instead of me, you become the lovers' bard.
And on each card, you hand paint for me a different bloom:
a giant peony, an Eglantine rose, foxgloves, a Brazilian plume.

99

On the writing desk, a picture of my late mother
tasting mushy food before feeding her baby – *me* –
wearing a little blue hat and a bib, looking eagerly at her.
We are in Parque Pereyra, an idyllic park of oak trees.
Mother is in a bright red dress, bathed in sunshine.
This is the only photo framed of her, and on its yellowed
back, some scribbles for her as I grew up, a few lines
when I was ill or missed her. *¡Mamá, te extraño hasta el cielo!*
The fast-eroding picture of a simple Autumn day
outside the city. What was it that she was thinking
as she was about to feed me, and what did father say
before taking the photograph, standing there, just looking?
And what happened next? Did she sing to me as I dozed
off reluctantly? And what did she see as my eyes closed?

100

In the recurring dream, I go back to Buenos Aires,
father (still well) waits in his impeccable yellow car.
At some point, we talk about the hot weather; he carries
my presents-filled bags. It is as if I see it all from afar.
The journey from the brand-new airport is too ominous,
the radio presenter talks fast, or is it me the one talking?
Something is not right. The Argentinean sun, monotonous.
I should know this place well, but somehow I'm straying.
At some point, (long dead) mother makes an appearance,
she has brought me her salami sandwiches for the road
and sweetly asks me how my life is going. No coherence
in this rolling dream, but a lingering taste of something odd.
When I finally wake up I'm always at a loss. Where am I?
I'm back home, of course. Still, outside, the strangest sky.

Notes

9: A reference to the Argentine soldiers who fought during the Falklands War in 1982 and burrowed for days underground like the armadillo, as referred to by writer Rodolfo Enrique Fogwill in his book *Los Pichiciegos* (1982).

20: Aleixo Garcia (?-1525) was a Portuguese explorer and conquistador in the service of the Spanish Crown. Some of his travels are told by Charles E. Nowell in 'Aleixo García and the White King', *The Hispanic American Historical Review* (November 1946).

23: In the Qom language, 'the one who is hard to destroy or kill'.

24: *The World Encompassed by Sir Francis Drake* is the earliest detailed account of Francis Drake's circumnavigation, including his encounters with various indigenous communities around South America. The book was compiled by his nephew Francis Drake and published in 1628.

29: More on Magellan's travels in South America in *The First Voyage around the World, 1519-1522: An Account of Magellan's Expedition* by Antonio Pigafetta.

33: From *Diaghilev's Empire: How the Ballets Russes Enthralled the World* by Rupert Christiansen (Faber & Faber, 2022).

34: Ulderico Schmidt (1515-1581) was a German soldier and adventurer who joined Pedro de Mendoza's expedition to the Americas, searching for personal fame and fortune. After twenty years, he returned to Europe still poor. However, he finally earned some money by publishing, in German, a book called *Voyage to Río de la Plata and Paraguay* in 1554. In this book,

Schmidt presents a series of vivid images that would influence all future representations of the region, describing the land as both populated and empty, fruitful and yet plagued by hunger, disease and thirst, with indigenous people who were often fiercely savage but remarkably friendly.

37: The British Museum in London owns about 90,000 contemporary, historical, and archaeological objects from the Americas spanning over 12,000 years. Indigenous communities in South and Central America still contest some of these items.

39: More on the gated community of El Paraíso Verde in *Nietzsche's Sister and the Will to Power: A Biography of Elisabeth Förster-Nietzsche* by Carol Diethe (University of Illinois Press, 2007).

45: From *Butterflies and Moths in Britain* by Vere Temple, (B. T. Batsford Limited, 1946-7).

46: This ink and watercolour drawing, titled *Botanical Garden, 2021*, was exhibited at the art show 'Pablo Bronstein: Hell in its Heyday' held at the Sir John Soane Museum in London from October 6, 2021, to January 2, 2022.

47: More on the Jesuit mission across South America in *Land Without Evil: Utopian Journeys Across the South American Watershed* by Richard Gott (Verso, 1993).

51: From *Great City Plans: Visions and Evolution Through the Ages* by Kevin J. Brown (White Star Publishers, 2020).

53: *The Witch* is a 2015 folk horror film set in New England, US, written and directed by Robert Eggers. It stars Argentinean Anya Taylor-Joy in her film debut.

65: As mentioned in *Italian Journey 1786-1788* by Johann Wolfgang von Goethe (Penguin, 2009), W. H. Auden wrote as an epigraph for the book, 'Some journeys – Goethe's was one – really are quests. *Italian Journey* is not only a description of places, persons and things, but also a psychological document of the first importance.'

66: *The Voyage Out* by Virginia Woolf was published in 1915. E. M. Forster described it as 'a strange, tragic, inspired book whose scene is a South America not found on any map.'

67: American lepidopterist, zoologist, and palaeontologist W. J. Holland (1848-1932) achieved international renown for supervising the mounting of several casts of the sauropod dinosaur Diplodocus. Holland tells of his 1912 trip to Argentina to install a replica of a Diplodocus at the behest of Andrew Carnegie in his travel book *To the River Plate and Back* (G. P. Putnam's Sons, 1913).

69: Charles Darwin (1809-1882) wrote *The Voyage of the Beagle* after five years of travels, including in and around South America, when he developed some of his earlier theories of evolution through common descent and natural selection.

72: German polymath, geographer, naturalist, explorer and proponent of Romantic philosophy and science Alexander Von Humboldt (1769-1859) wrote *Personal Narrative of a Journey to the Equinoctial Regions of the New Continent* between 1799 and 1804 after travelling extensively in Venezuela, Cuba, the Andes, Mexico and the United States. Humboldt is seen as the father of ecology and the father of environmentalism, although many indigenous people of Central and South America contest these claims.

81: The painting *After the Battle of Curupaytí* (*Después de la Batalla de Curupaytí*), created by Cándido López in 1893, hangs at the Museo de Bellas Artes in Buenos Aires, Argentina. This is one of the first paintings I saw as a child in a museum.

87: *The Purple Land* is a novel of 19th-century Uruguay by William Henry Hudson, known in Argentina as Guillermo Enrique Hudson. He was an Anglo-Argentine author, naturalist, and ornithologist who lived as a boy near Quilmes, the southern suburb of Buenos Aires where I grew up.

91: After the death of Argentine poet and short-story writer Jorge Luis Borges in 1986, he was buried in Geneva, the city where he grew up as a boy. His tombstone was adorned with replicas of historical artefacts, like a Viking ship and ancient Norse warriors preparing for battle. The carvings are surrounded by lines of text in Old English and Old Norse praising bravery.

92: *Alexander von Humboldt and Aimée Bonpland at Mount Chimborazo, Ecuador* was painted by German artist Friedrich Georg Weitsch in 1806. Between 1799 and 1804, Humboldt and his team of naturalists were led by indigenous guides through present-day Venezuela, Colombia, Peru, Ecuador, Cuba and Mexico, concluding their trip in the United States. Humboldt ascended Ecuador's Chimborazo volcano and analysed currents in the Pacific Ocean. Here, the German artist depicted a scene of Humboldt and his fellow traveller, Aimée Bonpland, standing at the base of the imposing mount.

94: Argentinean poet and anthropologist Néstor Perlongher (1949-1992) wrote *Corpses* (*Cadáveres*) during Argentina's bloody dictatorship and eleven years before his death from AIDS. The poem became one of the representative works of a Latin American postmodern poetry movement dubbed Neobarroco, *Neo-Baroque.*

96: Chilean writer, actress, scriptwriter and activist Nona Fernández (1971) published *The Twilight Zone* in 2016. Like the narrator of her book, she spent her childhood oblivious to the murderous policies of the Pinochet regime, responsible for over 3,000 dead or missing, for torturing tens of thousands of prisoners and driving an estimated 200,000 Chileans into exile.

Acknowledgements

Acknowledgements are due to the editors of the following journals where versions of some of these poems were first published: *POETRY*, *PN Review*, *Poetry London*, *Poetry Wales*, *Acumen*, *Firmament*, *Acentos Review*, *The Morning Star*, *fourteen poems*, the *Oxford Review of Books* and *The London Magazine*.

Several poems appeared in the following anthologies: *Mapping the Future: The Complete Works Poets* (Bloodaxe, 2024), *Bibliotech* (Paripe Books, 2023) and *Dancing About Architecture and Other Ekphrastic Maneuvers* (MadHat Press, 2024); Sonnets 31 and 32 were featured in *A Queer Latinxs Poetry Reading* (2023), a film directed by Vasco Vieira and commissioned to celebrate the 70th anniversary of The National Poetry Library, London.

Sonnet 30 'The Unholy Family' won the Keats-Shelley Prize 2019, judged by Michael Rosen, Deryn Rees-Jones and Will Kemp. 'A Latin American Sonnet LXXV', which appears as sonnet 68 in this collection, was highly commended in the Gregory O'Donoghue International Poetry Competition 2022, while 'A Latin American Sonnet XCV', appearing as sonnet 1 in this book, was commended in the Oxford Poetry Library competition 2024.

I want to express my sincere gratitude to my editor, Sarah Howe, for her insightful feedback, continuous support, and valuable suggestions during the editing process. I'd also like to thank the entire team at Chatto & Windus. I am indebted to the individuals who reviewed earlier versions of this manuscript, including Clara Farmer, Rosanna Hildyard, Mimi Khalvati, Pablo Bronstein, and Nathalie Teitler. My appreciation also extends to Michael Schmidt, who published the first sonnets in *PN Review*. I am also grateful to the Latinx community in the UK and beyond for the endless inspiration and friendship. I thank my family in Argentina and my extended family in London. Most importantly, my partner, Pablo, who is my first reader and other half, and my sisters Vero and Mari, to whom this book is dedicated.

Permissions

Excerpt from 'Sunstone/Piedra de Sol' by Octavio Paz in *Sunstone*, translated by Eliot Weinberger. Copyright © Octavio Paz, 1957, 1987, and Eliot Weinberger, 1987. Reprinted by permission of New Directions Publishing Corp. The same excerpt from 'Sunstone/Piedra de Sol' in *Collected Poems 1957–87* by Octavio Paz, translated by Eliot Weinberger. Copyright © Octavio Paz and Eliot Weinberger, 2001. Reprinted by permission of Carcanet Press Limited.

Excerpt from 'Third World/Tercer Mundo' by Cristina Rivera Garza, from *The Oxford Book of Latin American Poetry: A Bilingual Anthology*, translated by Jen Hofer. Copyright © Cristina Rivera Garza, 2009 and Jen Hofer, 2003. Reprinted by permission of Oxford Publishing Limited.

Excerpt from 'From the traveller we have . . .' by Cristina Peri Rossi from *State of Exile: 58*, translated by Marilyn Buck. Copyright © Cristina Peri Rossi and Marilyn Buck, 2008. Reprinted by permission of City Lights Books.

Index of first lines